Enchanting Tales of Sky the Cockapoo

Volume I

Amir R. Gill

AuthorHouse™ UK
1663 Liberty Drive
Bloomington, IN 47403 USA
www.authorhouse.co.uk
UK TFN: 0800 0148641 (Toll Free inside the UK)
UK Local: 02036 956322 (+44 20 3695 6322 from outside the UK)

This book is printed on acid-free paper.

ISBN: 979-8-8230-8329-4 (sc)
979-8-8230-8328-7 (e)

Print information available on the last page.

Published by AuthorHouse 06/23/2023

authorHOUSE®

Gratitude

First and foremost, I would like to thank the Almighty God and my Saviour, Lord Jesus Christ, for everything that I have in my life.

Next, I would like to pay tribute to my late mother, Mrs Elizabeth Peter Gill, who inspired me to be the person that I am today. By writing this book, I hope I may be able to continue her legacy of caring, compassion, forgiveness, tolerance, and storytelling. I hope key messages in this book may help inspire young minds to be literate, caring, and responsible, and loving towards each other and all creatures, great and small.

I would like to thank my siblings, Amber, Alia, and Imran, for their unconditional love and for giving me an amazing childhood. I would also like to thank my sisters-in-law, Jasmine and Sheeba, and my late brother-in-law, Anslem.

I would like to express my fondest love for Danzel, Sherry, Zion, Joshua, Eliza, Joel, Rielle, and Tara—my gorgeous princesses royale, the youngest and hence prettiest of them all—for making me such a proud uncle. I love you all and am forever thankful for having you in my life.

A huge thank-you to June (my adopted mum), John, Grant, Anne, Clint, Karen, Richard, Ruby, Dan, Mitchel, Isla, Asa, Anne, David, Fasih, Robert, Samantha, Vikki, Sofia, Aster, Chloe, Shane, Noman, Shoaib, Tim, Jennifer and many, many, more for their company, love, guidance, and support during different stages of my life.

I would like to thank my teachers, colleagues, and extended family members across the globe who made this journey called life a memorable one.

Finally, to my gorgeous boy Sky, who has given me so much love and joy. My darling Sky, because of him I have been able to overcome the grief of losing my mum, Elizabeth, due to COVID-19.

Sky is a true inspiration. I have tried my best to capture some of the greatest moments I have lived with him as a puppy dad. These moments, which I call Puppy Tales, are short stories that may inspire young minds to see life through his puppy eyes. The aim of this book is to offer inspiring messages for children and to commemorate all forms of life.

I sincerely hope by reading this book, children may learn to celebrate all forms of life and to have hope, love, care, and compassion for all living beings.

Enjoy reading!

With fondest love,

Amir R. Gill

How I Came to Be

In a small English town called Retford in Nottinghamshire, my parents—a gorgeous English cocker spaniel named Mini, and a French poodle named Teddy—fell in love and gave birth to us, a litter of five gorgeous, fluffy, and intelligent cockapoo puppies.

You must be wondering what a cockapoo is. Let me tell you, my reader friend of a humankind —a cockapoo is a hybrid of two lovely doggy parents. My gorgeous mum, Mini, an English **cock**er spaniel, and my handsome dad, Teddy, a French **poo**dle.

There were five of us pups, three boys and two girls. I was the eldest and the most mischievous of all. The fastest, the chubbiest, and the one with sparkly hazel-green eyes. My silky, fluffy champagne-coloured coat completed my cuteness in others' sight. This made me feel rather special as I received the most cuddles from everyone on our caravan site.

At the time of our birth, I was called Sparkly Eyes. My younger brother, who was born two minutes after me, was called Cuddly Hoot for crying aloud at his birth.

My second brother was called Mighty Muncher for having a big appetite and an attitude. He started munching Mum's breasts to feed as soon as he arrived.

My third sibling was a girl with a heavy, curly coat who was called Curly Clot. My fourth and youngest sibling was also a girl, and she had the longest eyelashes amongst us all. She was called Lottie Lash.

We lived happily in our wooden home on a caravan site with a pair of two-legged creatures of a different kind. They were smart and fast and took care of us without being asked.

We were happy and blessed for having each other and for having everything without begging or stress.

A Union of different Creatures – A Family

When I was eleven weeks old, I asked my dad what kind of creatures these two-legged beings were on our caravan site. My dad explained, "Oh, my darling boy, these two-legged creature are of a humankind, my fluffy bundle of joy. They are family as they love and care for us on this caravan site."

I asked my dad, "How come they are family as they are of different heights, have fewer legs, and aren't as furry as us in my puppy sight."

My dad said, "Ignore the differences that I could see through my puppy eyes." He told me to be a happy puppy and enjoy every day that we had together as a family on this caravan site.

My dad said, "one must learn to appreciate all that we have to make this journey called life a great adventure and a delight."

My dad explained that a family was not necessarily a clan of the same kind—we could ignore any differences if our hearts were aligned. "So, enjoy every moment, my fluffy bundle of joy, my cute little boy."

I learned that a family is not necessarily by blood or of the same kind. In fact, a family is a union of creatures who love, care, and protect each other throughout one's life.

The Male Two-Legged Creature of a Humankind

The male two-legged creature was called George. He was a grumpy, strong man who stood rather tall.

He was also loud, rushing and gushing in and out and here and there on our caravan site.

When he was eating his delicious shepherd's pie, he was kind of sly for not sharing his precious pie. Oddly, when we managed to steal the leftovers of his tasty pie, he howled and growled like a wild bear bragging his might as if he was the alpha male on our caravan site.

I paid him back for not sharing his tasty pie by chewing his slippers. He chased me for that, so I hid from his sight.

George was a good man, I must confess. He was our human friend, a hardworking carer who met our needs by setting out dry hay and clearing poo in our playground. He wanted us to have plenty of clean space to run around, though he moaned a lot when we caused havoc after messing around again in the playground.

I paid no attention to his moans, acting as if I was better than anyone grown.

I sneaked in his room and followed the smell of his dirty socks. I ran away with his socks and showed my siblings how great I was. I must say that chewing his socks was a great delight—a mischief I would remember for the rest of my life.

George looked for his socks and screamed out loud, which made me nervous. I said, “I am the prince of this doggy kingdom, you cowardly man; find and pick on a creature of your own size!”

He told me off again when he found me pulling and chewing the bog roll that he had placed high above on the wooden shelf, out of reach of my puppy eyes.

George yelled again, “Maggie, get this joker away of my sight so I can poo peacefully.” He sighed.

We all loved him really, and our play fights were a kind of family fun, to everyone’s delight.

The Female Two-Legged Creature of a Humankind

On the other hand, the female two-legged creature named Maggie was the one I liked the most. She was not only a carer but a great being and a lovely host. She gave me loads of doggy treats and played with us during the day whilst George was away.

My mum, Mini, often asked me to give them both loads of hugs and plenty of kisses—a doggy way to say, "Thank you, dear Mr and Mrs."

Maggie and George made me feel rather precious—oh yes, they did. This made my siblings envious of me due to their puppy crushes.

Maggie brushed our coats every day and provided water and treats to ensure we had a great day. I loved it when she cleaned my fluffy coat and removed pieces of hay that got stuck to my fur during play.

Maggie was a great cook. I could smell her cooking from a distance and asked others to invade her tiny kitchen, where a chubby tabby cat called Merlin stayed.

Merlin was a mean cat and was always a grump. She was a kind of maverick —the only one Maggie allowed in her kitchen. So, I tried my best to get on with Merlin in exchange for scraps of human food without being caught.

Maggie was not in favour of me having any human food. Her excuse was always that it was harmful to my health and livelihood.

"Maggie, oh Maggie," I said, "why don't you give me a piece of your delicious cheesecake? Why are you so mean?" Little did I know as a pup, she was doing this to preserve my health.

She shared no salt, sugar, grapes, chocolate, or raisins. Her excuse, as always, was that she wanted to preserve my gorgeous fluffy hair.

"Maggie, oh Maggie, this is not what I expected from your care. How can you not share a small piece of that scrumptious chocolate cake, the smell of which often fills the air?"

She said, "My darling Sparkly Eyes." She didn't offer me a piece because she cared.

Maggie said, "There are some foods that are harmful for puppies." Learning to avoid these was a test for which I must be prepared. She said that one day I would understand; it wasn't easy to raise a puppy, so I should consider myself lucky that she genuinely cared.

This didn't stop me trying my luck; I was often a nuisance. But now I know it was for the best.

I now know I cannot be offered all food that was prepared. For my health and wellbeing, I have learned to say no to everything toxic that could lead to a doggy hospital stay.

The Day of My Adoption

It was a bright morning in late May 2022 when Maggie gave us pups a bath, brushed our coats, and made us ready for the day. I asked my mum what was so special about this day. Mum said it would to be memorable and that I must behave and do as they say.

Little did I know it was the day to say farewell to everyone here; our days of playing together as siblings were coming to an end—sad to say.

Late morning, I saw through the corner of my puppy eyes as a pair of two-legged creatures of humankind came in a fancy car and took my sisters away. My mum had no time to say goodbye; she cried out loud and prayed, “Look after my girls, you kind people; keep them safe, and make sure they eat and stay warm and healthy and don’t end up as strays.”

This left us three boys with Mum and Dad, who were feeling sad and kept us close throughout the day. In the late afternoon, another fancy car pulled up, and there he was, a pleasant fellow who came over to us boys and said he was here to take one of us away.

I really liked him and walked closer to him, as he smelled so lovely. His smile attracted me to him, so I chose him and gave him a kiss to say, “I am ready, dear sir; please choose me and take me away.”

He lifted me up and hugged me gently. He said, “If you want to be my baby, I surely will take you away.”

I liked him even more when he let me say goodbye to everyone. He was so gentle and spoke with such care. My mum was happy and said, "You go with this nice man, my darling boy, and brighten his days."

He held me up in his arms and said to my mum, "I promise to take care of your boy; thank you for choosing me to be responsible for his upbringing and future care."

He named me Sky and said, "I promise you, Mini—he is my boy now. I will take care of him, so please don't worry or despair."

I felt happy and secure in his arms when he kissed me and said, "You are my Sky. I will be your puppy dad, and you will be my gorgeous little puppy boy."

I made an eye contact with this gracious man and instantly knew he would be a great daddy, so I stopped worrying and calmed down. I thought, *Life will be different from here onwards. I am heading to my new home, where I will live happily ever after, grow up, and play forever.*

He took me to his fancy car, placed me next to him, and drove away. He stroked my head and said, "I am Amir, my darling Sky. You will love your new home, where I am the lord of the manor, and you will be Sky Lord Junior, my pretty boy. So, relax and enjoy your first car journey; we are a family now, and we're going home to live in our manor in Chesterfield, Derbyshire."

When we arrived, he took me out of the car and wrapped me in an old towel that smelled of my mum, dad, and siblings, who were now so far away.

He kissed my head and said, "Welcome to your new home, my darling boy. Let's get you into your forever home, where you will grow up and I will grow old and grey. This is our home, so don't worry or cry. I am your daddy; we will have so much to do, make some happy memories, and play forever."

My New Home

My daddy opened the front door and brought me into this lovely manor he called home. I looked around and saw that everything was clean, tidy, bright, and warm.

He put me down and said, “Welcome home, Sky. There is so much to explore, so go on, my boy—wander off and get to know your new home.”

I followed my daddy in the kitchen and saw a lush green garden through the patio door where I could play. My daddy let me out in the garden, and I ran around silly on a bouncy bed of grass instead of dry hay.

My daddy said, “This is all yours, my gorgeous puppy boy. Go and explore your new home, my fluffy bundle of joy.”

He fed me delicious pieces of roast chicken with broccoli, carrots, and peas. I enjoyed my first dinner so much that I said, “Thank you, Daddy, for this. How lovely of you to bring me here. I love my new home; what a joy to be here with you in this haven where I would now stay.”

My daddy hugged me and said, “You are welcome; it’s all yours. I am glad you are here to stay. We will be happy here now; let’s make this house a home for both of us to be safe and happy for rest of our days.”

My daddy gave me loads of squeaky puppy toys as gifts and a new fluffy, comfy bed to sleep in. I wanted to be next to Daddy, so I started leaping towards him and wagged my tail for him to pick me up and play. My daddy smiled and picked me up. He gave me a hug and said, “Come on, little one; it’s time for sleep, not for play. You are welcome to sleep next to me, but you must sleep so that you can wake up fresh as we have plans for the next day.”

My daddy's bed was so comfy and bouncy. I worried I might topple over and fall away. My daddy saw I was nervous and gave me another hug. I loved it so much; I gave him loads of kisses for making me feel secure, loved, and special in every way.

I was so happy lying next to Daddy, and it was as if all the stress of the strange day was lifted away. I fell asleep and saw my doggy family in a dream. I waved happily at them and said, "Farewell, everyone. I have found a new daddy and a lovely home for my forever stay."

My First Day in My Garden

The following morning, I peed on Daddy's luxury satin quilt without warning or a say. Unlike George, my daddy cuddled me and said, "don't you worry, my little boy; it's a pee stain that can easily be washed away."

I was delighted and began to play. My daddy said, "No play on an empty stomach. Please eat your breakfast —smoked salmon with broccoli, peas, and carrots, which has been especially prepared to give you a good start for the day."

I gobbled it all down quickly and said, "Thank you, Daddy. I enjoyed my delicious breakfast. It had given me so much energy. May I now go into the garden to play?"

My daddy said, "Now that you have eaten, you may go in the garden to play."

It was a bright, sunny morning. I sniffed around, peed everywhere, and started digging young plants. That was fun and great play.

My daddy saw me digging and said, "Please stop digging young plants, my dear Sky. These were living beings that I planted to give our garden a gorgeous floral display."

I listened to my daddy and started playing with my squeaky toy instead. The noise of my squeaky toy attracted a blackbird that lived in my garden. He was black all over, with a shiny yellow beak, which he showed off during his noisy song and feathery dance display. The blackbird flew down to the garden shed and said, "Greetings, young one. Who are you, and why have your appeared so suddenly without any earlier news of your arrival been given away."

I replied, "Hello, Mr Bird. I am Sky, and my daddy brought me home yesterday evening. Didn't he say?"

The bird replied, "Hello, Sky! What a gorgeous puppy you are. It's a pleasure to meet you. I am Mr Knight, and I live in the oak tree. Welcome to our beautiful garden. Don't dig out plants that your daddy planted for a floral summer display."

As we were talking, a small bird with a squeaky song joined the discussion. The bird said, "Hello, Sky! I am Robina the Robin; I live here too. We are neighbours, so we must respect everything that your daddy has planted to make this garden a home for many living creatures. Some are shy and prefer dwelling behind foliage to remain hidden away."

All this noise attracted a chubby black cat from next door, who jumped up on the fence and shrieked, "What an awful way to wake up a sleepy cat. Don't you have something better to do, noisy creatures? Be quiet and shush. I need rest to unwind and to enjoy the glorious sunshine."

Mr Knight replied, "Hello there, Meow. Meet Sky, our new neighbour who moved in with his daddy yesterday."

Meow looked at me and said, "I see a rather fluffy and chubby pup—not too big or ferocious for a predator like me to take on and slay."

I jumped towards the fence to tell Meow, "I have claws and fangs too. I would fight back. I may be little, but I have a daddy who would skin a cat if I was threatened. So, keep away and don't complain later that I didn't say."

Meow laughed sarcastically. “I am a cat known to eat puppy tongues for supper. Don’t act smart with me you little pet. Do yourself a favour and stay out of my way.”

Meow lived next door with Alex and Sophie. When they heard the commotion taking place in the garden, they came to see what was happening. I saw two human heads pop up behind Meow. They introduced themselves, and Sophie said, “What a lovely puppy to have around!”

My daddy joined the gathering and introduced me to everyone as Sky Lord Junior. I felt happy and proud, so I sat in my daddy’s lap and grinned as if to say, “No one has a daddy as good as mine, so back off, Meow—I am here to stay.”

Meow noticed my pride and said, “Here is my daddy, Alex, you silly pet. My daddy is stronger than yours, and he would fight—I only have to say.”

My daddy replied, “Peace, everyone; we are neighbours, and we must learn to live happily. No one is greater than anyone else. What makes us great is how we care for, respect, and treat one another.”

Alex and Sophie agreed with Daddy, and Alex said, “Let’s not be spiteful, Meow. Sky lives next door, so stop being a bully, and don’t you let us down in any way.”

Mr Knight, Robina, Meow, Sophie, and Alex gave me a warm welcome that morning. Oh boy, I loved that moment so much that I filled with joy.

I just loved being the centre of attention. I surely was glad to have a daddy and a home with lovely neighbours of different kinds for daily chatter and play.

My First Visit to the Vet

My new home had so many gadgets and machines that I knew nothing about. I asked Daddy what these frightening beings were. My daddy smiled and said, "These are electronics to make life easier and keep everything clean."

I hated the noise of the vacuum cleaner and ran around frantically, as if this mean machine was attacking me. My daddy laughed and told me to relax and that it was a gadget to keep our flooring and carpets clean. He assured me I shouldn't be scared and should live this life of luxury without any care.

Later that day, my daddy told me to get ready to visit a vet for my health check. I asked Daddy, "What is a vet?"

My daddy explained that a vet was a puppy doctor who would check my health and would give me some treats if I did as he said.

My daddy fastened a glossy red harness onto me; it was comfy and a great fit, and it had a matching lead to compliment my new look. "A great choice, Daddy," I said and beamed as if I was the crown prince of England wearing his royal armour to show-off and be seen.

Meow was sitting in her window hatch and asked where I was heading looking so smug. She sounded curious and a tad upset.

I said, "We are heading to the vet."

Meow laughed out loudly and wished me luck. She said, "You go and visit the vet, you smartly dressed little pet. We all have this painful experience. It's your turn now. I would rather it be you than me."

I felt nervous and asked Daddy what Meow meant.

My daddy said, “Take no notice. Meow might be bored or can be an interfering little pest.” My daddy placed me in my new puppy car seat and fastened the seatbelt so I would be safe and relax.

A few minutes later, we arrived at the vet. A female trainee vet registered and weighed me. She asked us to sit in the waiting area—a crowded room with many furry pets waiting to be seen by the vet.

Everyone stared, making me feel awkward and scared. There were a few older dogs who laughed and said, “Hey, you pretty pup, why are you wearing a glossy red harness? Was this to intimidate, or is it a fancy puppy dress?”

My daddy said, “Don’t worry about what anyone says; you are special in every way. Others may try to put you down; remember to rise above and always be kind.”

A few minutes later, the vet called my name. We entered a room and met a vet called Fletch. He gave me a thorough check and discussed three jabs that were a must. My daddy said it would hurt a little and that I must cooperate for my wellbeing and puppy health.

Fletch brought three small jabs in a steel tray. Daddy placed me on the puppy stretcher so that it was easy for Fletch to administer these jabs in my bottom as I would lay. I yelled and almost bit Daddy’s hand. Daddy calmed me down and said, “Easy, my boy—a few seconds pain is worth it now to keep future infections away.”

I was a brave little puppy and took all three jabs on my bottom—what a horrible experience, I must say. I was sore, but knew my daddy was doing this for my health, so I obeyed.

We left the clinic with some flea drops and deworming tablets to take regularly to keep creepy crawlies and tummy worms away.

My First Visit to the Queen's Park

A week later, my daddy said now that I had my jabs, I was safe to visit local park for walks and play. I was scared and asked Daddy to carry me in his arms. I didn't want to walk a fair distance on my first day.

My daddy said walking on a lead was a doggy routine that I must rehearse and obey. This would help me grow and walk gracefully by Daddy's side; it would be a daily routine for the rest of my days.

I walked out with my glossy red harness securely fastened and the lead in Daddy's hand for my first walk on a sunny day. Walking beside Daddy was strange at first—a challenge I agreed to embrace to show I was a good boy in every way. I took little steps with Daddy despite being nervous. I showed respect and obeyed him all the way.

As we walked through busy streets, I witnessed many doggy breeds. To my surprise, there were many two-legged creatures walking side by side. Some had two-legged human pups, and some were walking their furry friends along the way.

Eventually, we made it to the Queen's Park. It was a lush green garden on a massive site. There were many dogs walking with their mums, dads, and carers. Some barked to scare me, and others simply walked past without a bark or a say.

In the middle of the park was a peaceful lake. I was excited to see many ducks and geese and even a pair of majestic swans swimming gracefully and quacking away.

In my excitement, I ran towards the lake and scared three cygnets who were resting a short distance away.

Suddenly, there was a whooshing noise, and a giant swan appeared from nowhere and showed his might with a great wing display.

He was huge and white as snow, with a long neck and a beak that scared me, so I jumped away. He said, "Back off, you little pup—my babies were resting. Why on earth did you interrupt their sleep and caused such unrest?"

I replied, "I am new here, Mr Swan. It's my first day at the lake. I am rather excited so please forgive me if I caused any unrest and scared your cygnets—this was not deliberate, I must say."

The swan mellowed and replied, "Oh well, since you have apologised and showed good manners and care, let me introduce myself. I am Major Cobs of the lake. I reside here with my wife, Mrs Pen, and my three little cygnets, Alfred, Meena, and Reena, whom you scared away. I am responsible for all feathery residents of this lake. I protect and care for all birds here, so be aware. No harm can come to them whilst I am here."

In response, I said, "Thank you, Major Cobs, for a great address. I am Sky, and I didn't mean to cause any upset, commotion, or unrest."

Major Cobs said, “Hello, Sky—what a marvel you are for showing, care, compassion, and respect.” He called out to all feathery residents of the lake for a quick hello and to avoid future scares and regrets.

I met a tufted duck, gadwall, mallard, teal, coot, pochard, wigeon, moorhen, shelduck, and a pair of visiting Canada geese. They flapped their wings for a warm welcome and said, “Greetings, young one; we hope you liked our feathery dance display.”

My daddy thanked Major Cobs and his friends. I felt wonderfully happy about having gained so many new feathery friends.

Major Cobs said, “Hats off to Sky’s daddy for raising such a lovely puppy boy with manners and etiquettes no less than royalty, I must say. You are welcome here any time, Sky. I see you are a well-mannered puppy and not a threat in anyway.”

On our way home, I said to Daddy, “What a wonderful world this is with a variety of beings. I wonder who the architect must be with such a skill to create beautiful beings different in every way. I am so pleased that I am part of this amazing world. I promise you—I will not take this life for granted. I will make something good of this journey called life by sharing love, care, compassion, respect, and honour to all living beings. I surely will convey this message of love, care, and tolerance wherever I go to make this world a better place for all creatures for the rest of my days.”

Printed in the United States
by Baker & Taylor Publisher Services